Campfire Capers

by Lisa Mullarkey
Illustrated by Paula Franco

Calico

An Imprint of Magic Wagon
www.abdopublishing.com

www.abdopublishing.com

Published by Magic Wagon, a division of ABDO, PO Box 398166, Minneapolis, Minnesota 55439. Copyright © 2015 by Abdo Consulting Group, Inc. International copyrights reserved in all countries. No part of this book may be reproduced in any form without written permission from the publisher. Calico™ is a trademark and logo of Magic Wagon.

Printed in the United States of America, North Mankato, Minnesota.
062014
092014

Written by Lisa Mullarkey
Cover illustration by Paula Franco
Edited by Rochelle Baltzer, Heidi M.D. Elston, and Megan M. Gunderson
Cover and interior design by Candice Keimig

Library of Congress Cataloging-in-Publication Data

Mullarkey, Lisa, author.
  Campfire capers / by Lisa Mullarkey ; cover illustration by Paula Franco.
    pages cm. -- (Storm Cliff Stables)
  Summary: Esha and her best friends, Avery, Bree, and Jaelyn, are set for a great summer at Storm Cliff Stables improving their riding skills--until Esha tells a ghost story around the campfire that has everybody jumping at shadows, and blaming the imaginary ghost for anything that goes wrong.
  ISBN 978-1-62402-049-0 (alk. paper)
1. Riding schools--Juvenile fiction. 2. Horsemanship--Juvenile fiction.
3. Storytelling--Juvenile fiction. 4. Best friends--Juvenile fiction. [1. Horsemanship--Fiction. 2. Storytelling--Fiction. 3. Best friends--Fiction.
4. Friendship--Fiction. 5. Mystery and detective stories.] I. Franco, Paula, illustrator. II. Title.
  PZ7.M91148Cam 2015
  813.6--dc23
                              2014005834

Table of Contents

STORM CLIFF
STABLES

"Scoot over," I said to Avery. "You're hoggin' the entire bench."

Avery inched over. "Esha, are you always this bossy or just at Storm Cliff Stables?"

Bree and Jaelyn laughed.

"You know me," I said. "Bossy and proud of it."

Jaelyn, Bree, and Avery are my best friends. We call ourselves the Core Four. We met here at Storm Cliff Stables four years ago. Jaelyn and Avery plan on makin' the US Equestrian Team. Not me. I ride to have fun. F-U-N. Bree used to ride but after gettin' thrown from her horse at home, she decided she was never ridin' again.

"Layla said this is going to be the best story ever," said Avery. "I hope it's not too scary."

Layla is one of our counselors. She's in charge of our cabin.

Bree looked around the campfire. "Where are the Pony Girls?"

The Pony Girls is a nickname for the new eight-year-old campers. They like to help Bree take care of all the farm animals. Bree teaches a barn rat class for them every day.

Aunt Jane overheard. "They aren't coming for another half hour. Layla felt this story was best suited for you older girls. I hear it's pretty scary."

Aunt Jane isn't my real aunt. She's the owner of Storm Cliff Stables. Everyone at camp calls her Aunt Jane.

After the openin' song, Layla jumped up on top of the picnic table. The glow of the fire reflected off of her face. She held up her hand and waited until everyone was quiet. The only sound you could hear was the cracklin' wood in the fire.

"On the quiet banks of High Point River," said Layla, "is a riding camp called Storm Cliff Stables."

I flared my nostrils at Avery and made a fang face. She rolled her eyes.

"A man named Crane was one of the stable hands here thirty years ago," said Layla. "Right, Aunt Jane?"

"Sounds about right," said Aunt Jane as she took a bite of her s'more.

"Just like we're doing now," said Layla, "the counselors would sit around the campfire telling all sorts of stories. But the scariest story of them all has never been retold. Ever. Until tonight."

"Why?" asked Jaelyn.

"Because it's a true story that will haunt you forever," said Layla. "Aunt Jane thought it would be too scary, but I convinced her that everyone here has the right to hear it. You need to know what could happen ... to you!" She put her hands on her neck, took a deep breath, and shuddered. "You might need to protect yourselves and your loved ones."

"She's a good actress," I said.

Bree raised her eyebrows. "Maybe she's not acting."

Avery bit her lip.

"Mark my words," said Layla. "You'll be so scared, you won't want to go to sleep tonight."

Avery whimpered.

"She's just kiddin'," I said. "No story's *that* scary."

Layla heard me. "This one is, Esha. It's a story about a rider who fought in the Revolutionary War. He had his head shot off by a cannonball. The rest of him was buried in an unmarked grave in High Point. That's the *real* reason Aunt Jane doesn't want anyone to go there."

Aunt Jane nodded.

Layla took another deep breath, both hands at her neck again. "It's been said that on nights when the moon is full, like tonight, his ghost appears and he gallops through Storm Cliff Stables looking for his head. He chases anyone he sees in hopes of getting a new head to use as his own."

Aunt Jane waved her flashlight around the fire, goin' from person to person. "He's not too picky. He'd take any one of your heads."

Everyone groaned. Avery inched closer to me.

Bree put her hands on her neck and whispered. "Is this a true story?"

"Layla wouldn't lie," said Jaelyn.

I laughed. "It's *just* a story."

Layla continued. "Crane was gullible. He believed every tale he was ever told. He was scared out of his wits when he heard this story, but Aunt Jane's cousin Rose told him not to believe everything he heard. For she was sure it was just a silly story."

Avery relaxed a little.

"Crane fell in love with Rose," said Layla. "Rose's father was one of the richest men in the county. Crane thought if Rose loved him back, he'd get a wife *and* a bunch of money here at Storm Cliff Stables."

"It's true," said Aunt Jane. "Every word of it."

Layla slowly shook her head back and forth. "Too bad for Crane though. Rose already had a boyfriend. His name was Brom. He was handsome. I should mention that he was a local farmer and was well liked by everyone. He had a great sense of humor and would play lots of practical jokes on his friends at Storm Cliff."

Aunt Jane stared into the fire. "At the end of the summer, under a full moon, the last big party was held at the Pavilion. Crane was excited because Rose had invited him. She was always nice to him and all the other workers. In fact, she was so kind to him that he decided he would ask Rose to marry him. He didn't care that she was spoken for. He bought a fancy suit and even borrowed a horse from a nearby stable so he could propose to her while on it."

Aunt Jane paused and looked each camper in the eye. "When Crane went to pick up the horse, he realized he'd have to go through High Point because the path up ahead was closed. So, he rode the trails and came to a long, rickety bridge. When he made it to the other side, he noticed the sun had set and the sky was welcoming a full moon. It was dark, and spooky shadows started forming around him from the rising of the moon. That's when . . . he remembered."

"Remembered what?" asked Avery, her voice shaky.

"The story about the Headless Horseman, of course," said Aunt Jane.

"He nudged the old horse to move faster," said Layla. "He was relieved when he could hear music and singing in the distance. And finally, the Pavilion came into view. He sure was glad to be off the trails. Once inside, Crane saw Rose dancing with Brom and tapped him on the shoulder. He wanted to cut in on their dance. But Brom refused to let Crane dance with Rose. Toward the end of the party, as Brom looked on with his friends, Rose told Crane she was now an engaged woman."

"That's so sad," said Bree.

Layla nodded. "At first, Crane was heartbroken. But that soon turned to him feeling foolish when he noticed Brom and his friends laughing in a corner of the Pavilion. He was sure they were laughing at him. So, he left and mounted the old horse. He was glad the full moon shone bright in the late summer sky so he could see where he was going. Without thinking, he took the same path back. But as he slowly plodded his way in the dark back through High Point, he remembered the same light he was so grateful for, was because of a full moon. And that full moon meant . . . "

"That the Headless Horseman was lookin' for a new head," I said.

"That's right," said Layla. "As Crane continued on, he thought he heard the sound of a horse behind him. But each time he glanced back, he couldn't see anything but blackness in the dense forest. He started whistling nervously. Then he urged the old horse to pick up the pace. It wasn't long before he thought he heard the sound of hooves following him again."

Aunt Jane cut in. "Within minutes, he was positive he could hear a horse gaining on him. He stopped just for a brief moment to reassure himself that his imagination was most likely playing a trick on him. But this time, he could make out a towering caped figure on horseback approaching him slowly through the trees. Crane's mouth dropped open as the shadowy rider came to an opening. An opening not fifteen feet away from him! The rider reached down to the ground and scooped up what looked like a head! A gigantic head!"

"With a bone-chilling cackle, the rider arched back his arm and threw the head," Aunt Jane continued. "As it hurled through the air, Crane realized it was not a head but a watermelon with flaming eyes. Crane begged his horse to go faster,

but the watermelon was thrown with such speed that it smacked Crane in the head and he fell to the ground. The Headless Horseman stood over Crane and pointed to his neck . . . "

"And then what happened?" Jaelyn asked. Her voice was shakin'.

But no one answered her. Layla just pointed up toward the sky. We lifted our chins to see the glowing full moon above.

Suddenly, Layla whipped her head around toward the dark trails. "What's that?"

There was a sound of pounding hooves coming from one of the paths. The gallopin' sound grew louder and louder until finally, a horse carrying a headless rider burst through the trees!

Everyone screamed.

I laughed. Couldn't they tell it was just a burlap sack tied over someone's head?

"The Headless Horseman!" yelled Layla.

Everyone jumped up to run, but no one wanted to look away from the Headless Horseman.

The rider slowly lifted a watermelon into the air and hurled it straight into the fire!

Avery screamed. Jaelyn prayed.

That's when Aunt Jane, Layla, and the counselors howled with laughter.

"Got you!" they said.

Layla ran over to the headless horseman and yanked the burlap sack off of him. It was Dr. Samuels, the camp veterinarian!

"Gotcha' girls!" he said. "I hope I didn't scare anyone too much!"

Everyone groaned. Avery rocked back and forth.

"Best. Story. Ever," said Bree. "No one can top that."

That's when I knew I had to try.

"Are you sure Layla's story about the Headless Horseman isn't true?" asked Avery at breakfast the next day.

I rolled my eyes. "I thought we settled this last night. This is the tenth time you asked me and the tenth time I'm gonna tell you it's not true. They retold *The Legend of Sleepy Hollow*. It's a classic story. Haven't you heard of it?"

She shook her head. So did Jaelyn and Bree.

"We read it in English class," I said. "At the end, you can pretty much figure out it was Brom playin' a trick on Crane. They changed the story so it took place at Storm Cliff Stables. They didn't use Crane's first name, either. It's Ichabod."

Avery let out a giant sigh of relief. Then she

laughed. "You should have seen your face, Esha, when that watermelon came flying through the air. You turned as white as a ghost."

"I wasn't scared," I said. "Just surprised."

"You weren't scared at all?" said Bree. "Not even an itsy-bitsy bit?"

"I knew it was someone playin' a joke on us." I bit into a muffin. "It was a good story. But not the best I ever heard. I've got a better one."

"Better than *The Legend of Sleepy Hollow*?" asked Jaelyn. "No way."

"Way," I said. "Mine's better because it's a real story. From India. My grandmother tells it to me every time she visits from India. After she tells it, strange things happen." I pretended a chill ran down my back and shuddered. "It creeps me out."

Avery dropped her fork. "Like what?"

"You'll have to wait until tonight to find out," I said. "Layla already promised I can tell it at the campfire."

Before I could say anything else, Aunt Jane's voice boomed over the loudspeaker.

"Attention, campers. We have a surprise for everyone behind the outdoor arena. Regular riding lessons will be pushed back thirty minutes so you can attend. Trust me. You won't want to miss it. See you in five minutes."

Jaelyn raised her eyebrows. "Maybe it's a visit from the Headless Horseman."

"Ha, ha," said Avery. "Very funny."

Bree picked up her tray and pushed in her chair. "There's only one way to find out. Let's go."

As soon as we walked behind the arena, we saw bales of hay forming a smaller, circular arena.

"When did they make this?" I asked.

Inside the center of the circle, Layla stood with Duke on a longe line. Everyone huddled in front of her, just outside the hay-bale arena. Within a minute, a woman came out into the center of the arena and stood behind Layla. Once Duke trotted around the circle a few times, the woman started to run side by side with him. Then she mounted him by liftin' herself high into the air and did a handstand!

"Wow," said Avery. "What an entrance! She made it look easy."

Within a few seconds, the woman grabbed onto some sort of saddle thingy and pushed herself up into another handstand. Then she started jumpin' and tumblin' all over Duke's back.

"What's she doin'?" I asked.

"I bet she's going to do a backflip," said Avery.

And she did! And not just one flip. For the next two minutes, she did all sorts of jumps and tumbles while balancin' on Duke.

"Amazin'," I said. "Is she a circus performer?"

Avery shook her head. "I doubt it. Haven't you ever seen vaulting before?"

Before I could answer, the lady did a backhand tuck to dismount and landed on the ground.

Everyone cheered. I cheered the loudest!

Aunt Jane held her hand up to quiet us down. "Don't spook Duke," she warned.

Then suddenly Aunt Jane ran next to Duke and jumped on him.

"Wow!" said Avery. "When did Aunt Jane learn to do this?" She inched forward to get a better view. "Watch this. They're going to perform together."

"No way," I said.

Bree laughed. "Way!"

Avery was right! Within a minute, the lady climbed up onto Aunt Jane's thigh and then did a front somersault landing in front of Aunt Jane.

I couldn't believe what I was seein'!

When it was time to dismount, they both did a cartwheel off of Duke and landed perfectly next to each other on the ground.

"Bravo!" whispered Avery.

"Bravo," whispered Jaelyn and Bree.

"Encore!" I yelled as I clapped and jumped up and down.

Bree poked me in the ribs. "Shhh . . . "

Aunt Jane had to catch her breath before she could speak. Layla gave her a bottle of water. Finally, she grabbed the microphone. "I started vaulting right after camp last year. But this is one of my friends and vaulting partners, Rebecca. She's been vaulting for six years now."

"Isn't she amazing?" said Aunt Jane. Rebecca is going to tell you all about vaulting, which is an official equestrian sport that's becoming quite popular in the United States. Starting today, you'll have the option of learning to vault here at camp if you want. It will replace one, or both, of your daily riding lessons. There are hundreds of clubs and competitive teams all around the country that you can join once you get some experience."

Rebecca stepped forward. "Hi y'all! Vaulting is an equestrian sport that combines dance and gymnastics on the back of a moving horse. Anyone can vault. I know all of you are experienced riders, but lots of new vaulters have never even been on a horse before. And don't worry if you've never taken a gymnastics class either. You don't need to do lots of fancy tumbles and jumps. But of course if you have gymnastics or dance experience, you'll most likely advance much quicker and compete at a higher level."

"It looks dangerous," said Bree.

Rebecca shook her head. "Vaulting is the safest equestrian sport out there. It's so safe that helmets aren't required. In fact, in competitions, they aren't allowed."

My ears perked up. I hated wearing my riding helmet!

"As you can see," said Rebecca, "during vaulting, a longeur is in control of the horse's speed. So, it takes teamwork to be successful. The longeur lets the vaulter stay focused on herself and the movement of the horse. Without the longeur's help, you wouldn't be able to stay balanced or safe on the horse."

"I took gymnastics before I started ridin'," I said. I pointed to Duke. "Can I try to do a back tuck off of him?" To prove how good I was, I stepped back a few feet and did a perfect back tuck. My feet landed exactly where they had started.

"Wow!" said Rebecca. "Impressive. What's your name?"

"Esha," I said.

Rebecca put her hands on her head. "If you did that on a horse right now, I'm afraid I'd have a heart attack. It would be too dangerous for a beginner. In fact, before you even sit and do one of the basic moves on a horse, you have to practice on a barrel horse."

A barrel horse? What fun is that? I clenched my

jaw as Aunt Jane and Layla carried a barrel on a stand over to the center of the arena.

"Why do I have to practice on *that* when I know I can do it on Duke?" I asked.

Aunt Jane sighed. "We're not in the business of breaking rules, Esha. Safety first." She walked over to me and put her hands on my shoulders. "Don't be so impatient."

"Don't worry," said Rebecca. "After you perform two of the mandatory moves on the barrel horse, you'll be able to try them out on Duke."

"When can I do flips and tricks?" I asked.

"That's called freestyle," said Rebecca. "Let's talk about that after you've proven you know some basics and can balance yourself on a moving horse."

Avery raised her hand. "How come no one needs to wear a helmet? Even the girls at the stable at home don't have to wear them while they're vaulting."

"Great question," said Rebecca. "Most of the time, vaulting is done without a helmet because they tend to get in the way. It can fall down over your eyes and block your vision. It can make you feel off-balance. They simply aren't designed for vaulting. Since the horse is moving in a circle, even falling is safer. There's a much smaller chance the horse will step on you."

Aunt Jane spoke next. "If you would like to take lessons today, you'll need to change into yoga pants or sweat pants. Take off your boots and wear either a double layer of socks or your sneakers. No riding boots, got it?" She glanced at her watch. "We'll meet back here in ten minutes." Then she added, "Can I have a show of hands if you're coming back?"

My hand was the first one in the air.

"Looks like fun," said Bree. "Good luck, Esha. I have to go muck out some stalls."

Jaelyn looked at her watch. "I don't want to miss my trail ride. I'm bringing my sketchbook."

Jaelyn was a great artist and never missed a trail ride. It was her favorite thing to do at camp.

"Maybe I'll do it with you tomorrow," she said.

I knew there was no way Avery would do it.

"Sorry, Esha," she said. "I really can't give up..."

"A jumpin' lesson," I said, finishing her sentence.

I curled my lip into a frown and pretended to be sad but I wasn't. For the first time, I could see myself winnin' a gold medal in the Olympics!

Rebecca made vaultin' sound so easy.

"Easy breezy lemon squeezy," I whispered into Duke's ear.

How hard could it be?

"Vaulting isn't an Olympic sport," said Rebecca. "Yet."

"What a bummer," I said. "Are you serious?" I kicked the ground. *Good-bye gold medal.*

"It could be one day," she said. "It's been featured in the Olympics for entertainment purposes twice so far but it's never been an official Olympic sport. But there are World Cup Championships. The competition is tough. The last World Cup winner was from England. She was only twenty-one."

I pointed to the barrel horse. "Do I really have to start on *that*?"

"Yep," said Rebecca. "But the good news is that I'm going to let you go first. Once you learn two of the mandatory moves, I'll let you practice on a real horse."

She had me start with a basic seat on the barrel.

"Sit on the barrel and hold your arms out to the side," said Rebecca.

"Like this?" I asked.

She nodded. "Raise your arms to ear level. Close your fingers and face your palm downward like this."

I copied her moves.

"Now arch your fingers a little like this," she said. "Point your toes down and arch those feet."

"No problem," I said as I flew through the moves. It was so super easy that anyone could do it.

"Good," said Rebecca. "Now I'm going to teach you flag position. You start from the basic seat position."

She showed me what it should look like. "Your turn."

I climbed back up on the barrel and sat in the basic seat position.

"Now hop up on your knees and extend your right leg straight out behind you." She held the position on Duke. "It's important to hold your leg slightly above your head so it's running parallel to the horse's spine."

As soon as I tried to get my leg parallel to the barrel, I wobbled.

Carly, a Pony Girl, laughed.

I stuck my tongue out at her which made me wobble even more. I had to hop off the barrel before I fell off. "Try it, Carly. It's harder than you think."

But it wasn't hard for Carly.

"Nice leg extension, Carly," said Rebecca. "Make sure your other leg distributes the pressure through your shin and foot."

When Carly looked confused, Rebecca pointed to her shin. "Most of your weight should be on the back of the ankle. This is so your knee doesn't dig into the horse's back."

Carly did it easily.

"Stretch your left arm forward," said Rebecca. "Position your hand the same way it was in a basic seat."

Carly smooshed her fingers together, faced her palms down to the ground and arched her fingers.

"Great job, Carly," said Rebecca. "Now make sure your right foot is arched and the bottom of your foot is facing the sky."

Carly looked like she had done this a million times before.

The other girls didn't have any problems either.

After everyone got a turn, Rebecca asked me to do it again. But each time I was supposed to move my right leg behind me, I wobbled. And each time, Carly smirked.

"Barn brat," I whispered as I got off the barrel.

"Hop back on, Esha," said Rebecca. "Concentrate. Vaulting is all about balancing yourself. You can't stay balanced or focused if you're too busy whispering to other vaulters. Look straight ahead. If you look down or try to sneak a look at anyone around you, you're going to wobble. Trust me."

So I tried again. This time, when I extended my leg, I didn't wobble. Not even a little.

"There you go," said Rebecca. "Nice and smooth. Now let's work on your other leg and arm."

I did exactly what Carly had just done. I didn't need Rebecca to coach me through it.

"Excellent, Esha!" said Rebecca. "A powerful flag stance. You can come down now."

As I got off the barrel horse, Rebecca gave me a high five.

Aunt Jane walked over with two more horses. "Are the girls ready to stand on a horse?"

All ten of us said yes faster than a horse eats a peppermint candy.

"You don't use a saddle on a vaulting horse," said Rebecca. "You use this instead." She held up some sort of seat and a thick pad. "It's called a surcingle, or a roller. You put it over this thick pad, which protects the horse. The surcingle has special handles. They help you perform certain moves. So do these leather loops you see here. They're called cossack stirrups. The horse wears a bridle and side reins. Look at Layla's longe line. Notice how it's attached to the inside bit ring in Duke's mouth."

Rebecca jumped up on Duke. "Once you get on the horse, bring yourself up to your knees while holding on to the surcingle. Then let go of it as you slowly bring your body up to a complete stand. Keep your arms out to your sides and bend your knees a tiny bit. It will help you stay balanced. If you don't bend your knees, your legs will start to get shaky and you'll fall."

Rebecca squeezed her hips and pushed her chest out a little. "Be sure to keep your upper body in line with your hips. Don't lean forward or you'll tip over."

Rebecca didn't wobble at all.

"It takes some time to learn how to stand," said Rebecca, "so don't give up if you don't manage to do it the first few times you try."

But I couldn't do it the first ten times I tried. Or the next twenty!

The girls from Cabin 3 could. Carly the barn brat could. Every other girl was able to do it except me.

"Practice makes perfect, Esha," said Rebecca. "You'll get the hang of it. Once you do, Duke will walk you around the circle."

"Can my horse canter?" asked Carly. "I have great balance."

Rebecca laughed. "You girls are certainly daredevils. Cantering is for those of us with years of experience. You'll start out with a walk and then advance to a trot when you're ready. It takes a long time to reach that level."

As everyone left to go to lunch, I stayed behind to practice on the barrel. I practiced through lunch and even signed up for the afternoon class. By the time five o'clock came, I was able to stand on a real horse while he walked around the circle!

"Good for you," said Layla. "You stuck with it. I knew you could do it."

As I grabbed my bag to leave, I saw somethin' shiny on the ground near the barrel. It was Carly's earring. I smiled as I shoved it into my pocket. *Perfect*, I thought. *Perfectly perfect*!

At dinner, I couldn't stop talkin' about vaultin'. "You should have seen me. I was able to walk twice around the circle without losin' my balance!"

"That's great," said Bree. "But wasn't Duke tired?"

"Duke went back to the stable at three o'clock. I practiced on other horses."

"Why didn't they let you take Queenie?" said Bree.

"I bet I know," said Avery. "Queenie gets spooked easily. I don't think she'd like anyone standing on her or flipping off of her."

"You're right," I said. Avery was *always* right about horses.

"And she's pretty cranky on a longe line," said Avery. "Layla never has any luck with her. Says she's wild. Just like you, Esha."

"Wild child," I said. "That's me."

I kept on talkin' about vaultin' until we got to the campfire. That's when I stopped talkin' about horses and started talkin' about ghosts.

I waited 'til everyone gathered 'round the fire before I started. "My Daadi, which means grandma, told me this story when she visited from India. She swears it's a true story." I lowered my voice. "A long time ago in a village outside of Mumbai, which the English called Bombay, there were a bunch of robberies. Lots of valuables were taken. At first, no one knew who the thief was or how he got into the homes. But the older people in the village knew better. They knew there was no need to call the police. They knew it wasn't a thief that was takin' everyone's valuables. At least not a livin' one. It was a ghost. A ghost named Suraj."

I heard someone gasp. It was probably Avery.

"You see, on the street where the robberies took place, there once stood a rich, prestigious horse academy known as Lord Oliver Ridin' Academy. The richer families from Mumbai and some of the British families sent their children there. They wanted them to become skilled riders so they could enter equestrian competitions. The poor people in the village weren't allowed to visit the academy or ride any of the horses. Instead, they were paid to muck out the stables.

One boy from the village, Suraj, loved horses. He wanted to become a skilled rider but wasn't allowed to take the lessons he needed. As a stable boy, he had to work long hours. He was surrounded by horses he could never ride. He was angry at the rich people for not sharin'."

"So what happened?" asked Carly.

"Late one night while workin', Suraj came up with the idea to steal things from the rich boys in the academy. He stole some watches and cuff links and sold them to a local man in town. He hoped to get enough money to pay for his admission into the academy. As time went by, he stole more and more from the rich. But he became too greedy. One night, a day after the full moon had lit up the entire city, Suraj decided he would steal one of the horses and sell it. But he chose a horse that had a bad temper. When Suraj mounted him, the horse became frightened and bolted away through the gates and over a nearby bridge. It was here where Suraj fell off the horse and disappeared into the Dahisar River."

"That's so sad," said Avery. "Did he drown?"

I shrugged. "He was never seen in the village again, but no one knows for sure. Now, my Daadi tells me that on the seven nights followin' the full moon, it's best to lock your doors and hide your valuables. If not, the ghost of Suraj will steal all of them hopin' to get enough money to gain admission into the long forgotten Lord Oliver Ridin' Academy."

"I don't believe you," said Avery.

"You should," I said. "Because before I came here, my Daadi called me and told me she saw Suraj and he was comin' to America this summer. Do you know why?"

No one said a word.

"Because Storm Cliff Stables is the most famous ridin' school here, and he wants the chance he never had to finally become a skilled rider."

Out of the corner of my eye, I could see Aunt Jane tryin' not to laugh. "This is a pretty expensive place for Suraj. How will he get the money he needs to stay with us?"

"He's goin' to steal whatever he can," I said.

I paused for dramatic effect.

"So tonight, when you're sleepin', you may see a ghost in your cabin lookin' for valuables to steal. And if you aren't extra careful, he may try to steal you, too!"

Everyone was quiet. Except for Carly. She started to laugh. "My mother says ghosts aren't real."

"Really?" I said. "Because I think he just stole your earring."

Carly reached her hand up to her ear and felt around for her earring. Her mouth dropped open. "It's gone!"

Now it was *Carly* who turned as white as a ghost.

"You really scared everyone last night," said Bree as she sat up in her bunk. She stretched her arms and yawned. "I don't think Avery slept at all."

Avery poked her head out from the bathroom. "I didn't. I kept looking for Suraj. I bet Carly didn't sleep either."

I thought of Carly standin' on Duke. Wobble-free right from the start. "Layla said Carly is one tough cookie. She isn't afraid of anythin'," I said. "She'll be fine."

But the truth was I hoped I did scare her. At least a little bit.

"She looked scared," said Jaelyn as she slid her feet into her riding boots. "I mean, you said you saw a ghost take her earring. I'd be scared."

I smiled. "I told you my story was way better than Layla's, didn't I?"

"Is it a true story?" asked Bree. "Come on. Fess up."

I crossed my fingers behind my back. "True story." Then I looked at the clock. "Hey! Why are you still here? It's almost eight o'clock."

Usually this time each day, Bree had already fed the farm animals, mucked out at least ten stalls, and groomed and tacked some of the horses.

"Because I was up late planning an activity for the Pony Girls," she said. "Besides, Aunt Jane ordered me to sleep in one day a week. Today was my day."

Aunt Jane had asked Bree to teach the Pony Girls all about being a barn rat.

Bree reached under her blanket and pulled out a notebook. "I made up a fun quiz about horses." Her face lit up. "Can I try the questions out on you?"

"Me?" I asked. "Take a quiz for eight-year-old girls?" I shrugged. "Sure."

Bree looked down the list. "Oh, you'll ace this." She cleared her throat. "How many blind spots does a horse have?"

That was easy! "Two," I said. "One behind the tail and one right in front of the nose. That's why you should always approach a horse from the side. You want to make sure it sees you. If you're in a horse's blind spot, you could startle it."

"Cor-rect," said Bree in a teacher voice. "Does a horse have a good or bad sense of smell?"

Another no-brainer. "They have a great sense of smell. Way better than ours. They can smell other horses in their herd a half mile away." Then I waved my hand in front of my nose. "Then again, I can smell your stinky sneakers from *ten* miles away!"

Bree folded her arms. "Ha ha!" She ran her finger down the page. "What is the sensitive, wedge-shaped part of a horse's hoof called?"

"Ribbit. Ribbit," I said. "It's called frog!"

"Cor-rect," she repeated. "Okay, try this one. It's another easy one but the girls may not know it. How many hours a day does a horse sleep?"

I thought about Queenie. *Doesn't she sleep when I sleep?* "Eight!" I said. "Everyone knows you need eight hours of sleep a night."

"Good one, Esha," said Bree. "Come on. Tell me the real answer."

Um . . . that was my real answer. I smacked my lips. "Too easy," I said. "Ask another."

Avery threw her pillow at Bree. "Everyone knows they only sleep for three to four hours a day, Bree. Although I think Sapphire sleeps even less than that."

Sapphire was a chestnut Thoroughbred mare that Avery rode every chance she got.

My face felt like it was on fire. "Yep," I said. "Everyone knows that."

Everyone but me.

I grabbed the notebook. "Come on, Bree. Get up! Get dressed! I want to eat."

Bree yawned again. "Stop being so bossy," she said. "What's the rush?"

"The sooner I eat, the sooner I get to vault," I said. "I'm really excited about it. I think I'm gonna be really good at it."

While Bree got dressed, I peeked at the rest of the questions. Out of the ten listed, I didn't know three! Maybe even four!

"It does look like fun," said Avery.

"What looks like fun?" I asked as I tossed the notebook onto the desk.

"Vaulting," said Avery. "Carly told me it was easy." She grabbed the book and turned to the questions. "These are going to be way too easy for Carly."

My whole body felt hot. Great! Not only was Carly a better vaulter than I was, but she was smarter, too.

I grabbed my bag that had Carly's earring in it. "Carly is a barn brat. Right, Bree?"

"She's okay once you take the time to get to know her," said Bree. "She's kinda cute. Layla said Carly reminds her of you *and* Avery. A great rider like Avery and bossier than you."

"Bossier than me?" I said. "Impossible."

But when I got to vaultin' class, I decided that Carly *was* way bossier than me.

"I'm first," she announced. "You guys have to wait until I go." Then she pointed to me. "Stay away from me. Go sit on the bench outside of the circle. I don't want to be near you in case Suraj is with you." Then she shook her fist in the air. "If you see that ghost, tell him I want my earring back."

I had to bite my tongue so I didn't laugh.

Rebecca spoke up. "Carly, I want Esha to go first. Have you warmed up and stretched yet? That's what the rest of you need to be doing. Esha's been stretching for twenty minutes already."

After proving to Rebecca that I remembered how to do a basic seat and a flag move, she let me stand on Duke's back as he walked around the circle.

"Remarkable," said Rebecca. "See how much you've improved already? Today, I'm going to teach you another move you need to know if you ever want to compete."

She showed me how to do a move called a mill on the barrel.

"From your basic seat position, bring your right leg over the horse's neck. You're going to have to let go of the grips and then grab them again once your leg is safely over. Now bring your left leg over the croup and be sure to release and grab the grips again. Then your right leg follows it. Next, move your left leg over the horse's neck to complete the full turn. When you compete, you'll have to finish each leg movement in four strides. Your legs must be perfectly straight. Don't bend your knees at all. Not even an inch. And it's important to point your toes. But we don't have to worry about that now while you're still learning."

I jumped up on the barrel and did the moves easily. It was fun when I got to sit backward.

"Excellent," said Rebecca. "Do it again. But this time, each time your legs are on the same side of the horse, press them together. No gaps."

So I did it again and pressed my legs together. "Ta-da!"

"Want to try it out on Duke?" said Rebecca.

"Already?" I asked. "Yep!"

She helped me get up onto Duke and as Duke walked around the circle, I was able to complete four mill moves on him!

"Super work, Esha," someone called out. "Impressive!"

It was Bree. She waved as she set her stuff down and walked over to talk to Aunt Jane. A minute later, Aunt Jane called over Rebecca.

I dismounted Duke and walked over to get some water. That's when I saw Bree's notebook with the quizzes sticking out of it. I looked them over. According to the answer sheet, every Pony Girl got all of the answers right.

I didn't want Bree to know they were smarter than I was, so I yanked the quizzes out of the notebook and shoved them into my bag.

I rubbed my hands together and smiled as I thought of my story last night.

Looks like Suraj has struck again!

Chapter 5

Fraidycats

At lunch, Bree searched through her bag and sighed. "I know I put them in here." She bit her lip. "I really wanted to see how much they learned."

Avery bit into her apple. "What's wrong?"

"I had the Pony Girls' quizzes in my bag. Now they're gone."

Avery gasped. "Are you positive you had them?"

Bree nodded. "Yep. Why?"

"It was him," I said. "Suraj!"

"No way," said Bree. "Why would he steal quizzes?"

"Way," said Avery. "We know he took Carly's earring. Now he's stealing from you. I bet he steals anything just to be mean."

Bree scanned the room. "Do you think he's here?"

Jaelyn laughed. "Come on, guys. Do you really believe Esha's story? I don't."

"Well, too bad for you," I said. "Because it's true. My Daadi told me."

I could tell Jaelyn didn't believe me so I turned to Avery and Bree. "I saw a shadow by the barrel today," I said. "It could have been him. But you weren't there."

"Yes, I was! I waved to you," she squealed. "Remember?"

I pretended that I had forgotten. "Oh, yeah! And it was 'bout the same time I saw that odd shadow." I wiped my mouth. "It was him. I just know it. I wonder what he'll steal next!"

A minute later, I knew the answer. When I went up to get some milk, I saw Aunt Jane's readin' glasses on her table. She was always losin' them and tellin' us she had to buy five pairs at a time. So as I walked back to my table, I swiped them off of her table and put them into my pocket.

This was the best joke ever!

But Aunt Jane wasn't laughin'. When we were inside the barn makin' scrapbooks, I saw her lookin' through Sapphire's stall. Then she went in and out of more stalls and muttered, "I know I had my glasses at lunch. Has anyone seen them?"

Carly touched her ear. "It's the ghost. Suraj has them."

"The ghost?" said Aunt Jane. She raised her eyebrows. "I don't think there's a real ghost, right Esha?"

"There is a ghost, Aunt Jane. My Daadi told me. Maybe he took your glasses."

Bree nodded. "I think he stole some papers from me."

"He took my earring," said Carly.

"I'm missing my toothbrush," said a girl from Cabin 3.

Toothbrush? Gross! I did not take anyone's toothbrush.

And then over the next five minutes, somethin' crazy happened! Everyone started blamin' Suraj for all sorts of things that went missin'. He was blamed for a missin' sweatshirt, a bag of potato chips, three quarters, a feather, the latest copy of *Horse & Rider*, a tooth that had fallen out, and a sock.

I flashed my fingernails to the group. "My orange nail polish was missin' when I went to use it today. Do you think Suraj took it to sell?" I acted upset.

Jaelyn looked bored. "Lucky for you that you have about ten more bottles of the stuff."

Aunt Jane clapped her hands together. "Girls! That's a lot of missing items. Did you ever just think that maybe you could have misplaced them? There has to be some logical explanation."

"There is," said Avery. "Suraj took them. If he didn't, then where is everything? Where are your glasses?"

Aunt Jane plopped down in a chair. "Good question." She looked at her watch. "At least I still have this. And it's telling me that your second round of lessons are in about five minutes."

I walked over to the circle arena by myself.

When Rebecca checked her clipboard she looked confused. "Carly? Has anyone seen Carly?"

One of her friends raised her hand. "She's not coming. She said she's too afraid to be around Esha because of her ghost story. She's going trail riding instead."

"That just means more time for us," I said. "The more time on Duke, the better. I really want to stand while Duke's trottin'. Think I can, Rebecca?"

But Rebecca wasn't listenin'. Four Pony Girls were tuggin' at her sleeve and givin' me the evil eye.

I moved closer so I could hear what they were sayin'.

"I don't wanna be here with her," said one of them. "I'm scared."

"If she's here, then Suraj might come here, too," said another.

"She's the one who told the story. It's her fault Suraj came to Storm Cliff!" said the third girl.

Rebecca held up her hand. "Girls. There's no such thing as a ghost. Especially one that comes to Storm Cliff Stables and steals from kids."

"And Aunt Jane," said one of the Pony Girls. "Suraj took her glasses, too."

Rebecca put her hands on her hips. "I can't make you stay for vaulting lessons, girls, but you're all doing so well. I think you should stay."

The girls finally quieted down. After a minute, Rebecca picked up her clipboard. "Okay! So it's settled. Everyone has decided to stay?"

The Pony Girls bobbed their heads up and down.

Rebecca looked around. "Has anyone seen my

good pen? It was just here a few minutes ago."

And faster than a horse tail swats a fly, the Pony Girls took off runnin' and screamin' as I slowly slid Rebecca's pen into my sock.

So for the rest of the day, I got to practice vaultin' on three different horses with just four other girls. I sure was glad those barn brats were such fraidycats.

I snuck back into the cabin before anyone else came back to wash up for dinner. I pulled my suitcase out from under my bed and unzipped it. I took Aunt Jane's readin' glasses and Bree's quizzes out of my bag and slipped them inside. Then I took Carly's earring out of my right pocket and Rebecca's pen out of my sock and tossed them into the suitcase too.

If only Rebecca knew! I laughed just thinkin' about the girls runnin' away.

As I was 'bout to zip up the suitcase, I noticed Avery's necklace hangin' up on the bulletin board. I walked over to it and held it up to the light.

It was a gold horseshoe that had diamonds in the gold. Sparkly! Whenever Avery needed good luck, she put on the necklace.

I held it up to my neck and looked in the mirror. It was beautiful! In the mirror, I thought I saw somethin' flash behind me.

I turned 'round. "Who's here?"

But no one answered back. I poked my head into the bathroom. "Anyone here?"

No answer.

I opened the closet door. "Anyone in here?"

No answer.

I looked in the mirror again and thought of Suraj. I shuddered. Not only did I scare a lot of the girls, but I was startin' to scare myself!

I took off the necklace and dangled it from my finger for a minute before placing it next to Aunt Jane's readin' glasses in the suitcase.

Chapter 6

Bad Luck

"I don't want to go to the campfire," said Avery. "Does anyone want to stay here with me?"

"*Skip* a *campfire*?" I asked as I glided polish across my nail. "Are you sick of s'mores already?"

Jaelyn twitched her nose. "She's afraid to hear more stories. You know, *ghost* stories."

Bree nodded. "I don't want to hear any more either. First the Headless Horseman. Then the story about Suraj. I'm all creeped out."

I blew on my nails. "The campfire's the best part of the day. Next to vaulting, that is! You gotta come," I said. I shoved my hand under Bree's chin. "Funky color, huh?"

Bree grabbed my hand. "Hold still. Let me see them."

"I did a pattern. Orange and green. Think they're bright enough?" I held up my pinky. "How cool is this? I used a black marker to write on it."

"Hmm . . . #1 Vaulter?" said Bree. "Cute!" She looked at her own nails. "Maybe I should paint mine and write #1 Scaredy-Cat because I really don't want to hear any more scary stories."

"You don't have to worry," said Jaelyn. "I heard Aunt Jane talking to Layla at dinner. She said there's no story tonight. Said something about needing a break from it."

"Really? No kiddin'?" I asked. "What a bummer. The girls in Cabin 3 said they had an even scarier story than mine. Not that I think that's even possible. But still." I sighed. "I really wanted to hear it." I tightened the lid on the bottle and tossed it on my bed. "Guess we'll just have to wait until tomorrow night."

So, without worrying about scary stories, we left for the campfire. The walk didn't take more than five minutes. We always walked single file down the windin' trail even though the path was big enough for all of us to walk next to each other. Jaelyn led the way.

As I followed the beam of her flashlight, I could see a glow up ahead and the flicker of flames through the branches. As I got closer, I heard the cracklin' and snappin' of twigs and logs. I took a deep breath. *Nothin' beats the smell of a fire.*

When we got there, it was already crowded. Everyone was sittin' 'round the fire on benches. The counselors were busy settin' up the s'mores station, tunin' up their guitars, and readin' over scripts.

Aunt Jane banged a pot as she climbed on top of the picnic bench. "Good evening Storm Cliff Stables campers!" She let out a huge *neigh* that sounded exactly like Queenie's when she was excited.

We gave her an even bigger *neigh* back!

"Layla and I got to talking at dinner," said Aunt Jane. "We've decided we're going to change it up tonight. So, we'll still have our songs, a skit, and oodles of s'mores, but we're going to skip the scary story."

Some kids cheered. Others booed. I booed the loudest of all.

"Come on now, girls. We simply don't have time for stories about ghosts and headless horsemen tonight."

Avery shook her head. "Did she even have to *mention* him?"

"We don't have time because we decided everyone needs to relax a bit more tonight. So we're having Movie Night under the Stars!"

Everyone cheered.

"Are we having popcorn?" asked Carly.

"We're popping it now, Carly. But you Pony Girls don't know what's so special about our

Movie Nights under the Stars." She glanced around the fire. "Esha! Want to fill them in?"

"We get to bring our horses out at night," I said. "They hang out with us and we braid their manes and tails."

The Pony Girls went wild.

"Don't forget to grab your brush from the barn in case you feel like grooming your horse, too," said Layla. "I think they'd appreciate the extra attention." She pointed to two trees with a white sheet hangin' between them. "We have the movie *Misty* to show you. I think it's a movie you campers and your horses are going to love!"

"Aunt Jane and Layla are the best!" said Avery. "My favorite nights are when she lets us bring our horses here."

"I agree," said Bree. "And I'm so excited to see *Misty*. I loved the book *Misty of Chincoteague*."

"Me, too," said Jaelyn. "My parents promised me we're going to visit the horses on Assateague

Island. The pictures of the horses roaming free are amazing."

"What do you mean roamin' free?" I asked. "No stables? Who owns them? Who takes care of them?"

"Half of Assateague Island is in Virginia and half of it is in Maryland," said Jaelyn. "The sides are separated by a fence. In Virginia, firefighters own the herd of horses. They take care of them and give them shelter. Once a year in July, they auction off some of them to raise money. But in Maryland, no one really owns them. They can go wherever they want, whenever they want. I want to see them swim."

"That's so cool," said Bree. "Maybe we can all go to see them next year."

I felt sad thinkin' 'bout next summer. My parents just got divorced, and I wasn't sure where I'd be livin' next year. "Sounds like fun," I said.

Avery got up first. "Let's go get our horses

before the movie starts."

Bree jumped up. "I'm going to the barn to get Pip. I hope Squeak doesn't feel left out."

Pip and Squeak were two of the cutest miniature horses at Storm Cliff Stables.

Jaelyn was excited. "I braided Blue's tail today. Maybe I'll try some fancy braiding on his mane tonight." She rubbed her forehead. "Unless my headache gets worse."

"Who are you bringing?" asked Bree.

"Queenie, of course," I said. "Who else would I bring?"

Jaelyn looked surprised. "I thought you'd bring Duke. You've been spending so much time with him while vaulting."

"I miss Queenie," I said. "I haven't groomed her or even visited her much in the last few days."

"Don't worry about her," said Bree. "Carly rode her yesterday and today. Helped put on her tack, too."

My stomach felt funny. Part of me felt bad for ignorin' Queenie over the last few days and part of me was mad at myself for feelin' so jealous of an *eight* year old.

When I got to Queenie's stall, Carly was already there.

"I'm bringin' Queenie," I said. "You better find another horse, Carly."

"I just stopped by to give Queenie an apple," she said. She put her hand under Queenie's mouth but pulled it away as soon as Queenie stretched her neck to eat it. She tried again. This time, the apple fell to the ground.

"Give me the apple," I said. "There's nothin' to be afraid of if you do it right. But if you do it wrong, Queenie will bite you. Not because she's mad or anythin'. But because you stuck your fingers in her mouth. You don't want to do that, got it?"

"Got it," she said.

"Try it like this," I said. I placed the apple in the palm of my hand. I made sure my fingers were touching each other and pulled my thumb in tight. I flattened my hand and placed it about five inches under Queenie's chin. She bent over and brushed her fuzzy lips against my hand and lapped up the apple.

"Good girl!" I whispered.

Once Queenie lifted her head up, I pulled my hand away and rubbed her neck.

"She likes it," said Carly.

I reached into a bucket and pulled out another piece of apple. "Now you try it."

It took a few tries, but Carly finally understood what to do.

"I had a hard time the first few times I tried to feed a horse, too," I said. "I was scared."

Carly's mouth dropped open. "*You* felt scared?"

"Yep. Everyone gets scared about somethin' once in a while," I said.

She nodded and leaned in close to me. "I'm sorta scared right now. I'm afraid I'm going to see Suraj and cry."

Now I felt bad. And once I saw her eyes fill with tears, I felt really bad. Really, really, really bad.

I was just about to tell her the truth when Layla interrupted us. "Carly, Duke's ready." She handed Carly the lead rope.

"Coming?" asked Layla.

"Just need to get my groomin' brush for Queenie. I'll meet ya there in a few minutes."

Five minutes later, just as I was leaving the stable, I heard a scream comin' from the cabins. Then I heard voices. I turned Queenie 'round and walked toward the cabins. That's when I heard Avery screamin', "The ghost took it! Suraj was here!"

Her necklace!

Chapter 7
Another Thief

I stayed hidden behind some trees but close enough to the path that I could hear what Avery was sayin' to Aunt Jane and Layla.

"It's gone," said Avery. "My lucky necklace is gone."

"Are you sure?" asked Layla. "When's the last time you wore it?"

Avery leaned on the porch railing. "Two days ago. I took it off before I showered and hung it up on the bulletin board. That's where I always hang it. I wanted to show Sapphire while we watched the movies. I'm jumping my highest jump ever tomorrow so I really need the luck." She put her hands on her head. "Now it's gone."

"Are you sure you tacked it up onto your

board?" asked Aunt Jane. "Maybe it fell behind the desk."

Avery shook her head. "I looked. And I'm positive. Positively positive I hung it up. I always do." She lowered her head. "I looked all over the room."

"Well now," said Aunt Jane. "Let's not be so glum. Come to the movie and try to have a good time. We can look for it tomorrow when the light is better. It's so dark out here. Unless you're by the fire, you can't see much."

"What if the ghost took it?" said Avery. "Suraj could be selling it right now."

"I don't believe in ghosts," said Aunt Jane. "Don't you think Esha made up her story?"

"I believe her," said Avery.

I was still hidden when Avery led Sapphire past me. When she sniffled as she passed, I knew I had to get the necklace back to her. Pronto!

"What if someone stole it?" I heard Layla ask

as she walked by. Then she stopped about five feet away from me. "Have you seen the necklace? It's horseshoe shaped with diamonds outlining the horseshoe. It's not only beautiful but I imagine it cost a lot of money."

"Who would steal it?" asked Aunt Jane. "A worker? A camper? I don't even want to think about it." She sighed. "Let's not let our imaginations get the best of us." Then Aunt Jane scratched her head. "I'll tell you what, Layla. If anyone took that necklace for *any* reason, they'll be fired or sent home immediately. No questions asked. I won't tolerate that type of behavior here at Storm Cliff Stables."

Sent home?

I took a deep breath as I tried to figure out what to do. I was 'bout to go back into the cabin, when I saw a light inside turn on. Who was it?

Suraj?

My chest felt heavy and my stomach felt

jumbly. I wasn't 'bout to wait around to find out. That meant I had to go back to the campfire and face Avery. I crossed my fingers that she wouldn't still be upset when I got there.

But she was.

"Suraj stole it," she said. "I just know it."

"Um . . . I doubt it. I'm sure you'll find it tomorrow mornin'," I said.

She started to braid Sapphire's tail. "You think so?"

"Yep," I said. "I know so. I just have this feelin' it's gonna show up."

I'd make sure of it.

Then Avery started to cry. "My grandmother gave it to me. It was hers when she was my age. She wrapped it up and gave it to me last Christmas. And now it's lost." She blew her nose. "My parents are going to ground me."

"I bet you'll find it tomorrow," I said. "Your parents will never have to know."

I was just about to blab the whole truth to Avery when Layla came over to check on her.

"Are you okay, Avery?" She squeezed her shoulder. "I promise that I'll help you look for it in the morning. Bree and Esha will, too. Right, girls?"

Bree nodded. "Jaelyn, too."

"Where is Jaelyn?" I asked. I looked around.
"Is she here?"

Avery blew her nose again. "She went back
to the cabin. She wasn't feeling well. Her head
hurt."

So it was Jaelyn who turned on the light!

"I better go check on her," said Layla. "But I really came over to tell you not to worry. The necklace has to be *somewhere* here at Storm Cliff Stables. Necklaces don't just disappear."

"What if someone stole it?" said Bree.

Layla sucked in her breath. "Well, if someone took it for any reason, then they'll be fired, or, if it's a camper, they'll be asked to leave immediately."

"Immediately?" I asked.

"Immediately," repeated Layla.

I rubbed my head. Jaelyn wasn't the only one with a headache.

It wasn't long before all the other girls came over to find out what was wrong.

"I heard Suraj stole your ring," said one of the girls in Cabin 3.

"It was her necklace," said Bree. "And we don't know what happened to it."

"I'm missing my robe," said another girl. "I think Suraj took it."

"And my care package from home never came," said another camper. "But then I got to thinking. What if it *did* come and Suraj stole it?"

This was getting out of control.

Every girl who came up to Avery told her Suraj had stolen something from her, too.

Part of me wanted to tell everyone that *I* was Suraj. A thief. But if I did, I'd never see Storm Cliff Stables again.

I was glad when the movie ended. I wanted to climb into my bunk and figure out how I was gonna get Avery's necklace back to her without anyone findin' out that I was the one who took it.

But by the time we got back to the cabin, I was so tired that I fell asleep the second my head hit the pillow. And I didn't wake up until eight thirty! I missed breakfast! I sat up in bed. "What time is it?"

"Almost time for your vaulting lesson," said Avery. "Bree's down at the stable and Jaelyn is hiking to Keeter Falls. Remember?"

Jaelyn had been talkin' about this hike for a week. How could I have forgotten about it? "Did she bring her sketchbook?"

Avery nodded. "And her camera."

Then I remembered last night. "How are you?" I asked.

She shrugged. "Layla's right. My necklace has to be around here somewhere. I mean, it's not like it could walk away. Unless . . . "

I hopped out of bed. "Unless what?"

"Unless Suraj came and stole it," she said.

I couldn't take it anymore. "Suraj didn't steal it, Avery."

"How do you know?" she said.

"Because I made up the story," I said. "I wanted to scare everyone. I wanted to have the scariest story ever at Storm Cliff Stables."

She started to brush her hair. "Yeah, right. You just don't want me to freak out. I know it's a real story, Esha. I believe you."

"No, really," I said. "I made up most of the story."

But when I looked at Avery, I could tell she didn't believe me. There was only one thing I could do. Prove it to her.

So while Avery went to the bathroom to brush her teeth, I reached under the bunk and pulled out my suitcase. She would be surprised. She'd have to believe me now!

But I was the one who was surprised. When I opened the suitcase, it was empty!

Chapter 8
Feeling Guilty

I quickly zipped up the suitcase and shoved it back under my bunk. *What happened?* Not only was the necklace gone, but so was everything else.

Avery walked back into the room and stared at me. "What's wrong, Esha? You look like you've seen a ghost." Then she snorted. "Please tell me you didn't see Suraj."

I didn't know what to say!

"Well," she said, "what's wrong? Spill it."

"Nothin'," I said. "I was just hopin' that you might have dropped your necklace on the floor. But I looked under the bunks and I don't see it anywhere." I stood and brushed some dust off of my pajamas.

"I already looked under there last night," said Avery. "I think I looked *everywhere* last night. So I was thinking maybe I lost it in the stable. Or in the Pavilion." Then she grabbed her sweatshirt and opened the door. "Thanks, anyway," she said.

"For what?" I asked. If she knew what I had done, she wouldn't be thankin' me.

"For trying to make me feel better," said Avery. "You didn't have to say you made up the story but I appreciate it." As she was leavin', she added, "I'll see you at lunch! Hopefully, I'll have my necklace back by then."

As soon as she left, I grabbed the suitcase and threw it on my bunk. *Please let me see her necklace when I open it up.* I closed my eyes and counted to three. *One, two, three.* But when I peeled back the lid, it was still empty.

I scratched my head. *How could everything vanish?* It didn't make sense. Or did it?

I thought about Suraj. An awful feelin' came over me. *What if Suraj really did come to Storm Cliff Stables and steal from me?*

I thought of tellin' Aunt Jane the truth. And I almost did until I saw her at vaultin' lessons.

"How's Avery?" she asked. "I really hope we find that necklace. I'd hate to think what will happen if I find it on another camper. Or worker."

I felt like throwin' up. "She's okay," I said. "I mean, I guess she's okay."

Layla came into the circle. "I just saw Avery. I got her to smile but I do have some bad news. She's with Sapphire."

"Why is that bad news?" I asked.

"No," said Layla. "The fact that she's smilin' and is with Sapphire is good news. But she just told me she won't jump Sapphire today. Or tomorrow. Or any other day until she finds her necklace."

I opened my mouth to tell them everything that had happened, but the words wouldn't come out.

Then Layla looked at Aunt Jane's hands. "You're not wearing your rings today."

Aunt Jane held out her hands. "Nope. Can't."

Layla bit her lip. "Please don't tell me they're missing. Don't even say the word Suraj in your next sentence."

I held my breath. I was thinkin' the same thing!

Aunt Jane smiled. "Nope. I'm cleaning them. I know exactly where they are."

They both laughed. But I didn't. How could I? Once everyone knew what I had done, I was gonna get kicked out of camp for stealin'.

As I was debatin' what to do, Rebecca came into the circle. "Did you tell them, Esha?"

I froze. How did Rebecca know? I shook my head from side to side. I could feel my face gettin' red.

"Don't be so shy," said Rebecca. "I'll tell them."

I squeezed my hands together and held my breath.

"Esha has really nailed everything I've taught her. It's only been a few days, but I can tell this is her sport."

"Really?" I said.

Aunt Jane and Layla laughed.

"Don't look so surprised, Esha," said Aunt Jane. "When we decided to bring vaulting to camp last week, we did it with you in mind. Right, Layla?"

She nodded. "Yep. It's perfect for you, Esha. I have this funny feeling you'll be competing before long."

"Well she can't compete unless she can learn how to mount the right way. So, that's what I'm going to work on today. Are you ready for the challenge?"

Even though I nodded, I didn't think I was ready. *How could I concentrate on vaultin' with Avery's necklace missin'?*

But I didn't have a choice. Before I knew it, Rebecca had me practicin' a basic mount on Duke.

"The goal is to get onto the horse while making it look easy," said Rebecca. "You'll have to nail down the basic vault-on before you can try to increase the difficulty with fancy mounts."

"How many different ways can you mount a horse?" I asked.

"There are *dozens* of ways," said Rebecca. "The easiest is the basic mount. But I like to increase the difficulty during competitions. Sometimes I'll keep it simple and mount to a sideways layout on my stomach. But if I want to impress the judges, I'll mount to a full handstand. That took me a long time to master."

After two hours of tryin' to master just a basic vault-on, I didn't even want to think about any other fancy schmancy way to get up on Duke.

"Just remember to swing your right leg as high as possible," said Rebecca. "Your pelvis has to be higher than the horse's head."

I tried it again.

"You're almost there," said Rebecca. "Be mindful of the horse, Esha. You need to try to land a bit softer. A bit more graceful. And once you're in the seat, you need to keep your upper body vertical. Nice and tall."

Layla walked over to us. "Is something wrong, Esha? It looks like you're having a hard time today. It's not that we expect you to be able to perfect the mount yet. But you look distracted."

I didn't say anything.

"By not talking, you're just confirming that something's wrong. Where's bossy Esha today? The girl who doesn't stop talking?"

I pressed my head onto Duke's neck. "That's the problem. If I talk, someone's gonna be mad at me. Real mad."

"Friend problem?" asked Rebecca.

I thought of Avery. And Aunt Jane. "Yep. You could say that."

"You know what I always say?" said Layla. "Talking it out leads to working it out."

Layla handed me Duke's lead line. "Bring him back to the stable. Groom him and give him some treats. He deserves them." Then she softly patted my back. "While you're at it, give yourself a treat, too. You also deserve one."

I faked a smile as I walked Duke toward the stable.

"If she only knew," I whispered to Duke.

If she only knew . . .

As soon as I got to the barn, Bree waved me over to Queenie's stall. "I had a bucketful of apples and carrots in here today. Now they're gone. Do you think Suraj took them?"

That's when I started to cry.

"Esha! What's wrong?" asked Bree as she hugged me. "If he took them, it's okay. I can get more."

"I'm gettin' kicked out of camp," I said. "Because I'm Suraj."

Bree looked confused. "*You're* Suraj? What do you mean?" Then her eyes grew to the size of full moons. "And why would you be getting kicked out of camp?"

"I mean that *I'm* the one who took Carly's

earring. And your quizzes. And Aunt Jane's glasses. And . . . Avery's necklace."

Bree's eyes bugged out of her head. "You stole them? Why would you do that?"

I glanced around the stable. "Shhh . . . keep your voice down." I pulled her into an empty stall and closed the door behind us. "I didn't steal them. I *borrowed* them. It was just a joke. A stupid joke." I kicked some hay into the air. "But now the joke's on me."

Bree paced back and forth in the stall. I could tell she was thinkin'. Finally, she stopped movin' and put her hands on her hips.

"Why did you *borrow* them?" she asked quietly.

"So everyone would say that my story was the scariest one at camp this year. Once I told the story, it was easy to pretend Suraj was here. So, I started takin' things and I wanted everyone to think it was the ghost. I thought I was bein' clever. And funny." I leaned against the wall. "And you know what? I made up half of the story."

Bree's lips curled. "I hope you made up the part where Suraj said he was coming to America and heading straight here to Storm Cliff Stables."

I nodded. "Yeah. I made that part up."

"Why did you take my quizzes?" asked Bree.

"Because I was embarrassed. When you were gettin' dressed, I read the questions in your notebook. And I didn't know four of them. *Four* of them!" I shoved my hands in my pockets. "I didn't even know that horses only sleep for three to four hours a day. So when I saw the quizzes near the water station, I peeked at them. I saw the answer key and checked over each quiz. *Every* Pony Girl got them all right. I felt dumb. *Really* dumb. I didn't want you to know the Pony Girls are smarter than me."

Bree hugged me again. "Esha! I don't think you're dumb. I think you are one of the smartest girls here. And funniest. Who cares if you didn't know a few questions? It's not a big deal."

"It was a big deal to me, Bree," I said. "And when I took Avery's necklace, I had no idea her grandmother gave it to her. It means a lot to her and now it's gone forever."

Bree looked confused. "What's the problem? If you took it, just give it back to her."

"I would if I could," I said. "But I can't."

"Sure you can," said Bree. "It's easy. Just hang it back on the board. Or put it in the bathroom and let her find it."

"No, no, no," I said. "I can't give it back to her because someone stole it from *me!*"

Bree's mouth dropped open. "Someone took the necklace?"

I nodded. "And Carly's earring and your quizzes. Everything! They took everything. And if Aunt Jane finds out that I'm the one who took everything, she's gonna kick me out of camp!"

"No she wouldn't," said Bree. "Not if you explained what happened."

I told Bree all about hearin' Aunt Jane and Layla talkin' on the trail.

"And I was gonna give back the necklace to her this mornin'. But when I opened my suitcase, it was empty. Completely empty."

"You don't think . . . ," Bree covered her mouth. "I don't even want to say his name anymore."

"Suraj?" I asked. "Do I think Suraj is real and that he really came to Storm Cliff Stables to steal from all of us?" I said.

Bree bobbed her head up and down.

"Nah. No chance, Bree. That's the part I made up."

Bree was quiet again. She started pacing up and down the stall again. "I think I know who stole Avery's necklace from you. And all the other things."

"Who?" I asked.

"Jaelyn," she said.

Now my mouth dropped open. "*Jaelyn?*"

"It makes sense," said Bree. "She went back to the cabin with a headache. She was the only one who was in our cabin alone. And when I got back to the cabin, I saw her push a suitcase under the bed. The red one."

"The red one is *my* suitcase," I said.

"She told me I shouldn't be scared of Suraj because she *knew* the story wasn't true. But I didn't believe her." She looked at her watch. "Once she gets home from her hike, we can ask her."

"What should I do now?" I asked. "I hate lying to Avery. I feel awful about everything."

But Bree didn't say anything. Instead, she stood on her tiptoes and pointed to the door. That's when I saw Avery and Sapphire walking down the center aisle.

I took a deep breath and opened the door to the stall. I peeked out into the aisle and saw Avery goin' into Sapphire's stall. I followed her inside.

"Hi, Avery," I said. "We gotta talk."

Avery smiled and picked up a brush. She ran it over Sapphire's back. "Sure. What's up?"

I couldn't even look at her. I stared at the ground. "I did somethin' bad. Really bad. So bad that once you find out what it is, you're not goin' to want to hang around with me anymore."

Avery laughed.

"I'm not kiddin'," I said. "And once I tell you, I'm pretty sure I'm gonna get kicked out of camp."

"Esha, what are you talking about? You're one of my best friends. I'm sure whatever you did isn't a big deal." Then she added. "Unless it was you that stole my necklace." She made a ha-ha face and pretended to belly laugh.

But when she saw that I wasn't laughin', she grabbed my arm. "*You* took my necklace? Where is it?"

She looked like an angry hornet.

But when I told her the whole story, she wasn't mad.

"You're not mad at all?" I asked. "Not even a little bit?"

"As long as Jaelyn really has it, then nope. I'm not mad," said Avery. "I just want my necklace back." She fed Sapphire a carrot.

I felt so much better.

"But I do think you should tell Aunt Jane the truth,"she said. "If you don't, then we *all* have to lie for you."

"I'd lie for you," said Bree. "If it meant you wouldn't get kicked out of camp. I could say I found the necklace outside next to the cabin."

Suddenly, I felt worse. "No, Avery is right. I don't want all of us gettin' kicked out of camp."

Avery laughed. "Don't be so dramatic, Esha. Do you really think Aunt Jane is going to make you leave Storm Cliff Stables? You didn't steal the things to keep them. You pulled a prank. And I can admit it was a pretty good one now that I know I'm getting my necklace back."

"So you think she'll just laugh and forget about it?" I asked.

"Well...," said Avery. "I didn't say that exactly. I think she'll make you muck out the stalls by yourself for a week."

"Or make you work with the Pony Girls *every day*," said Bree.

I covered my eyes. "I think I'd rather get kicked out of camp!" Then I added, "Just kiddin'."

"Okay," I said. "I'll tell the truth. But I'm waiting until after the campfire. She's always in a great mood after she eats some s'mores."

We had to wait until after lunch to see Jaelyn.

As soon as she walked into the barn, I pounced on her. "Fess up. Did you take my things out of my suitcase last night?"

She looked at Avery, then Bree, and then me. "Yep. But they weren't your things. I knew your story wasn't true. I mean, come on. Out of all the stables in the world, Suraj just *happens* to pick Storm Cliff Stables? When things started disappearing, I thought it was funny. But when Avery's necklace went missing, that was too much. I knew she'd be upset so I wanted to teach you a lesson."

"But why didn't you give it back to me this morning?" said Avery. "I spent a lot of time looking for it today."

Jaelyn looked at Avery. "I wrote you a note explaining everything. I put it on your bed. Didn't you read it?"

Avery wrinkled her nose. "I never even saw the note."

Now it was Jaelyn's turn to feel awful.

"It's okay," said Avery as she held out her hand. "I don't really care what happened. As long as I get my necklace back, it's all good. Aunt Jane doesn't have to know anything. I don't like to lie to her, but I also don't want her to kick you out of camp, Esha." She tapped her outstretched hand. "Hand it over, Jaelyn."

Jaelyn slid her backpack off and unzipped it. "Sure thing."

She dug through it for a minute before she dumped out everything onto the floor.

Then her smile faded.

She whispered, "I can't give it back to you, Avery."

Avery put her hand down. "Why not?"

Jaelyn's whole body started shaking.

"Because I lost it!"

"Funny," said Avery. "Good one."

Jaelyn's voice squeaked. "I'm not kidding. It's not here."

Now Avery was mad. Steamin' mad!

"Where is it?" she demanded.

Jaelyn covered her face with her hands. "Oh no . . . "

"What happened?" I said. "Did you lose it?"

Jaelyn groaned. "I took out a snack to eat when we stopped at a waterfall. And when I took it out, I also grabbed my wristlet and sketchbook. And . . . "

"And what?" Avery said.

"And we saw some pretty birds in a tree," said Jaelyn. "So I started sketching them. And then we had to start hiking again. So I put my sketchbook into my backpack. But I must have forgotten to put the wristlet back in."

She looked through the pile on the floor. I could see the quizzes and Aunt Jane's glasses in the pile.

"I left it next to a tree," she said quietly.

"And my necklace is inside of it?" asked Avery.

Jaelyn nodded. "And Carly's earring."

No one said a word for a minute. But then Avery exploded.

"You lost *my* necklace out on a hike? In the middle of a forest? A *huge* forest?" She started to cry. "It was my grandmother's."

"I'm so sorry," said Jaelyn.

"It's not really *your* fault, Jaelyn," said Avery. She glared at me. "Esha's the one who stole it in the first place."

"But *I* didn't lose it," I said. "I had it in my suitcase. It's *Jaelyn's* fault."

Bree tried to calm everyone down. "It doesn't matter whose fault it is. The fact is that Avery lost something that was really special to her."

"The most special thing I have," she said. "*Had*, I should say."

"I have an idea," said Jaelyn. "Let's tell Aunt Jane. Maybe she can help us find it. It's by a tree near that small waterfall up at Pine Peak. I bet it's still there." Then she chewed on her lip. "I mean, I *think* it's still there." She scratched her head. "Or maybe it's by the stream. I'm getting confused." She shrugged. "At least I know it's next to a tree."

"*Next* to a tree?" said Avery. "Gee, that helps," she said. "There's only about a zillion trees out there."

"Sorry," Jaelyn whispered.

"I'm sorry, too," I said. "I really am."

"That doesn't help me get my necklace back," said Avery.

"Then what should we do?" asked Bree.

"I'm going to go find it," said Avery. "Right now. I've been cross-country riding up at Pine Peak with Layla before. It's only about two miles away. If I leave now, I can make it back before it gets dark outside."

"Are you crazy?" I said. "You can't go ridin' out there."

"You're right," said Avery. "But I can go hiking. Jaelyn can come with me to show me where she thinks it is. We could be back before anyone knows what we're doing or where we went."

Jaelyn nodded. "I'll go."

Bree looked nervous. "I've been to Pine Peak, too. I know how to get there. Want me to come?"

Avery shook her head. "If we all go, Aunt Jane will know we left camp. We'd be in big trouble."

Bree agreed. "Okay. But leave now before it gets dark. We'll cover for you here." She looked at the clock. "It's only three o'clock. We still have three hours before dinner and more before it gets dark."

"We'll be home in two hours," said Avery. She grabbed bug spray off of the bathroom counter and sprayed herself. Then she sprayed Jaelyn. "Let's go."

As they left, Bree shouted, "See you in two hours!"

But we didn't see them in two hours. Or three or four hours.

"Something bad has happened to them," said Bree. "I just know it."

I agreed. "Coverin' for them at dinner was easy. But Aunt Jane's gonna know somethin's wrong if they don't show up for the campfire."

Bree looked out the window. "It'll be dark soon. I think we should go look for them." Then she looked terrified. "But what if we get lost? I mean, I've been to Pine Peak before, but not in the dark. It's going to be creepy in there when it gets dark."

That's when I grabbed our flashlights and a

bottle of my nail polish. "We can't get lost with these!"

We snuck out of the cabin and walked to the trail that led to Pine Peak. Bree stopped at the edge of the trail. "It looks dark in there already. How are we going to find our way back?"

"Did you ever read about Hansel and Gretel?" I asked.

Bree nodded.

"They left a trail of bread crumbs so they could find their way home," I said. "But the birds ate the bread. Since the bread crumbs were eaten, Hansel and Gretel couldn't find their way back home. But we won't get lost with *this*!" I held up my neon orange nail polish. "We'll mark the trees with it. It glows in the dark!"

Bree jumped up and down and clapped her hands. "You're so smart, Esha! What a great idea."

"Smarter than an eight-year-old named Carly?" I asked.

"Smarter than all the Pony Girls combined," said Bree.

So as we walked into the woods, we used the polish to mark the trees. I put a splotch right at eye level on every tenth tree we passed. Below it, I drew a little arrow pointin' the direction we were goin'. This way, I knew we'd only be ten trees away from the next tree.

"It's a good thing we have the trees marked," said Bree. "Without that, I don't think we'd ever be able to find our way out of here."

We had walked about a mile when we heard two voices in the distance.

"It's them," said Bree.

We started shoutin' their names. "Avery! Jaelyn! Where are you?"

"We're over here," shouted Jaelyn. "We're lost!"

We had to walk over lots of fallen trees before we reached them.

"You're not lost anymore," I said.

"Are we glad to see you guys," said Avery. She held up the wristlet. "We found the bag at least two hours ago, but I think we've been walking in circles. We can't find the way back to camp."

"I don't think I've ever been so happy to see a wristlet," I said.

"Me, too," said Bree.

"Me, three," said Jaelyn. She looked exhausted. She turned to face Avery. "They probably don't know how to get back to camp either. It's getting hard to see anything. Pretty soon, it's going to be pitch black in here."

"That's okay," I said. "Because in less than an hour, we'll be at the campfire. Promise. We're only about a mile away from Storm Cliff Stables."

Avery looked worried. "But we keep walking in circles. How are we going to get out of here? I have no idea which way we should walk."

"Just look for Esha's nail polish," said Bree. "She marked lots of trees with it. So, we just need to follow the trees out of here."

Avery's eyes lit up. "Wow! What a good idea. That was so smart of you, Esha. I never would have thought of that."

Avery opened up the wristlet and took her necklace out. She dangled it in front of me.

"I'm so happy you found it, Avery," I said. "I promise I'll never touch it again."

"You have to touch it again," she said. "Don't you get it?"

I was confused. "Get what?"

"You're my good luck charm," said Avery. "If you didn't come find us and mark the trees, we could have been here all night."

She unhooked the clasp and told me to turn around. Then she put the necklace around my neck.

"Just for tonight," she said.

I smiled at her and touched the horseshoe. "Just for tonight. Promise."

As we walked back to camp, I told them all about vaultin' and how I really wanted to try out for a team when I got home.

"If I find a team, do you think I can borrow your necklace for tryouts?" I asked Avery. "I'd take real good care of it. Promise."

"I'd say yes," said Avery, "but I've seen you practicing. I don't think you need any luck. You're really good so far."

"Think so?" I asked as I saw the glow of the campfire up ahead.

"Know so," said Avery.

And for the first time, I believed it myself.